Reflections: Michigan 2015

An Anthology Celebrating Michigan

Lake Superior

Lake Michigan

Lake Huron

Edited by Evelyn M. Zimmer

For permission requests, write to the publisher:
"Attention: Permissions Coordinator", at the address below.
Zimbell House Publishing, LLC
PO Box 1172
Union Lake, Michigan 48387
www.ZimbellHousePublishing.com

© 2015 Zimbell House Publishing, LLC

Published by Zimbell House Publishing, LLC
www.ZimbellHousePublishing.com
All Rights Reserved

Print ISBN: 978-1-942818-02-1
Electronic ISBN: 978-1-942818-03-8
Library of Congress Control Number: 2015900454

Reflections: Michigan 2015

An Anthology Celebrating Michigan

Edited by Evelyn M. Zimmer

Reflections: Michigan 2015 is a literary journal produced by Zimbell House Publishing showcasing the talents of new American writers.

Within these pages are short stories celebrating Michigan. We hope you enjoy reading these new authors as much as we enjoyed bringing their new voices to you.

The top three winning submissions are:

First Place   Edward Ahern for *The Cottage*

Second Place   Caitlin Siem for *Off the Bluff of Big Bay*

Third Place   James Vescovi for *Harry & Stevie*

Acknowledgements

The production of this anthology could not be accomplished without the dedication and literary expertise of our Zimbell House team.

Our sincere thanks goes out to everyone who submitted for this anthology, for without you, there would be no new voices to tempt us.

Contents

After the Fall

By John Vicary

For three full months after the fall, Jem's mother cried herself to sleep. After that, she didn't shed another tear. It was as if she'd wrung herself dry from all that weeping. Years later, Jem thought the same thing when she sat, stony-faced, at her own sister's funeral and never so much as sniffled. But then he remembered those long nights during the move, and he thought maybe he understood.

Momma didn't cry when Metairie went under for the last time, either, but Jem did. It meant sharing his bedroom with his cousin Willie. "It was only a matter of time, honey," she said. "That place flooded in the best of times. We make room for family. We're lucky that we can."

That's easy for her to say, Jem thought. She doesn't have to sleep with Willie.

It *was* easy for her to say, then. Momma needed Aunt Arlene as much as Aunt Arlene needed a place to stay, since Daddy had left to find work. The house felt empty with just the two of them, and while Momma clucked her tongue and patted Aunt Arlene on the back, the lines around her mouth eased just the tiniest bit to have her sister near her again.

The lines on Momma's face returned when the tidewater of the newly renegotiated banks of what used to be Lake Pontchartrain crept north. Jem charted the course of the rising and receding, that primordial rhythm that only the moon could call, but for all his worry the water would have its way.

By the time Picayune fell, Momma must have known that Daddy wasn't coming home. There weren't any jobs in the South, and there was nothing to come home to, now, anyway. Jem would sometimes look west, into the setting sun, and he would imagine his dad in an apple orchard or maybe a lemon grove. He had no reason to think that Daddy worked with his hands or that he lived in the west. He didn't even know if they had lemon trees there, but it gave him comfort to imagine it, so he did.

"We have to leave here, Jo."

Jem could hear his Aunt Arlene through the thin plasterboard walls without listening very hard. It had never bothered him before; for years he'd heard his parents' murmured conversations, their words of love, the comforting susurration of their whispers and their companionable silences. Now he ached to turn away, but he was trapped between Willie and the wall.

"I can't leave my home!" Momma cried.

"I know how it feels. I'm so sorry, darling, but you know we can't stay. We'll make a fresh start. I have a friend in Detro—"

"You want me to live on charity? What's the matter with you?" Momma's voice grew louder.

"It wasn't charity when I came here," Aunt Arlene said. "It's people helping people."

"It's charity. I'm better than that!" Momma snapped.

"Oh, and I'm not? You think anyone likes this, Jo? You think I *wanted* to come here?"

Jem shoved his head into the pillow, but he could hear his mother's raised voice through the feathers. "It's just ... this isn't for me. I never thought I'd be in this position, that's all. We had a plan, Ken and I. We had a plan, don't you understand? It wasn't supposed to be this way."

There was a silence, and then he heard crying.

It didn't stop for a hundred days.

****

Winter had been the biggest change for Jem. He'd never seen snow before, but Detroit iced over with the stuff every October to May. He'd had to learn to breathe slowly so he didn't burn his lungs with the bitter northern air.

Momma didn't grow used to the seasons this close to the Arctic Circle. She refused to leave the apartment, even though the uncirculated air became stale with the odor of so many bodies. She saddened and sickened, her own inscrutable cycle much like the tides that drove her there. She stayed bundled in a tattered blanket in the corner between an elderly woman who reeked of piss and a man with a long beard who didn't seem to understand English. Jem didn't need to listen through walls now; at night, conversations swirled around him like wind through the cattails on the bayou.

"...trying to find my daughter..."

"They say in China..."

"I read that the bees are dying. Once they're gone, we're all dead. Dead as doornails, ayup."

"...hydroponics. It works, if you know the right plants..."

"I *said* you could use it! You don't have to ask again!"

"Hand pollination's the wave of the future, mark my—"

"Give it here."

"...try to put it in the window. The sunlight makes it grow."

The voices formed a lullaby mosaic, and Jem would sleep and tangle in his dreams of bees and floating plants in China. He wondered if it snowed there or if they had floods, too. He hoped that somewhere the sun was shining in a clear sky. Maybe he would visit someday. He imagined traveling all over the world with the man with the long beard until they found the country whose language he spoke. Jem had a recurring dream in which he stepped out of the plane to see fertile soil and houses with white fences still standing in front of every one. Jem smiled, wanting to stay, but he always woke up just as the man took his first step towards home.

The event that saved his mother came in the form of a muffled groan in the middle of the night. Momma never slept well anymore, and she was the first to hear Mrs. Levitsky laboring alone in 3D. By the time Momma knocked on the door, Mrs. Levitsky was already on her knees and crowning. After that, Jem's mother helped most of the women deliver their babies and in the process found, if not a reason to live, then at least a reason to stop crying.

On a rare night one August, they found themselves alone in the room. "I wished for so much more for you," Momma said. She stared, unseeing, out the busted screen into the cityscape of refugees.

Jem swallowed. "I know, Momma. But it isn't so bad here."

"How can you say that?" Momma turned to look at him. Her eyes were dry, but they brimmed with anguish. "Of course you say that. You don't know what you're missing. When I think of the years I spent growing up ... it was so different. I used to play in the grass. I used to sing and dance. I was so carefree. I never had to worry about this world, not the way that you do. You'll never see those days.

There's nothing for you here. What have I given you? What have we done to you?"

Jem took one breath, and then another. His life beat through his veins with every throb of his heart. Beyond the broken screen he could see the rainbow sheen of oil on the Detroit river glinting in the setting sun. It was beautiful. "I know, Momma," he said. "It'll be okay."

"Okay?" She barked a bitter laugh. "How will it be okay? Nothing will ever be okay again."

Jem tilted his head. A solo bird sang unseen in the dirty city. Its song filtered through the noise and reached them in the darkened tenement. "I met someone."

"What?" Momma sounded shocked. "Are you in love?"

"No." Jem smiled, remembering. "I was walking down Woodward the other day and I saw this flash of blue. It was the prettiest color. It reminded me of home. I followed it and it was a girl wearing a raincoat. I asked her to walk with me for a bit, just 'til I got to Cass. We talked about all sorts of things. She's amazing, Momma. I just had this feeling that it's all going to be okay. There *is* something for me here. I have you. And I have hope."

"Hope." Momma rolled the word in her mouth as if she were tasting it for the first time. "Hope."

"Yes," Jem said.

Momma said nothing for awhile. "The baby on the third floor died, you know. She came too early. Mrs. S something. Simms, I think. I didn't even know her name." She looked at her hands. "Hope."

Jem didn't know what to say. "I'm sorry, Momma."

"Don't be sorry." Momma straightened her shoulders as if she'd made a decision. "Don't you ever apologize for surviving—for living. For being young. This is how things are now, aren't they? We have to help each other now, more than ever. That's just how things are. We can't go back. Can we?"

"No, Momma." Jem answered, but he knew she wasn't really talking to him. She had a faraway look in her eye, but she seemed more present than she had been since the fall.

"That's a good boy. Listen, you find your girl and you invite her around here. Your Aunt Arlene and I will make her feel welcome. I'll have Willie fix up that broken chair." Momma looked around. "I need a shower. I just noticed."

Edited by Evelyn M. Zimmer   *Reflections: Michigan* 2015

Jem listened to the birdsong. He wondered if it was shining in China now and he smiled.

Blessed By Gitchee Manitou

By Caitlin Siem

In a time long ago, when demigods still ruled the lands the Great Spirit, *Gitchee Manitou*, blessed one with a daughter. Chief Sleeping Bear's daughter was the most beautiful woman to walk the land. When his daughter was born her beauty was yet to be seen, but as the girl aged and grew older her allure became more apparent. Once the girl was of marrying age word of her beauty swept across many nations and drove men to the Ottawa tribe in an attempt to marry the fair maiden.

Sleeping Bear grew furious with all of the attention his daughter received. He loved her more than anything and a fierce rage grew deep within him when he imagined these savage worldly men attempting to take her away.

"You are not worthy of these mortal men," Sleeping Bear said to his daughter. "Your beauty will cause a great grievance in the land, many wars will rise over you."

Doing the only thing he could, Sleeping Bear led his daughter to the great river, Third Fire, and placed her in a canoe that he tethered to a giant tree.

He helped his daughter into the boat. "I can keep you safe here. Each day I will bring you food. Except for when I am here, you must stay hidden."

"But father," said the girl, "I dream of running free in the meadows and through the woods. Please do not make me hide away from the world."

While it broke Sleeping Bear's heart to see his daughter sorrowful, rage filled him when she attempted to disobey his order. The Earth rumbled underneath them as his anger swept outwards. "You will obey me!"

With tears trailing down the girl's cheeks, she nodded and hid away from sight.

Each day, as promised, the chief brought food to his daughter and only at this time was she allowed to come out of hiding. She would anxiously await the tug that jolted the canoe when her father began to pull the rope toward land so that she may step out and be free for a moment.

While the demigod was able to protect his daughter from the pursuits of mortal men, there was another that started to take notice, one much greater than any man.

The Wind paid little heed to the canoe that floated in the river. Until one day, when the Wind was blowing through the area did it notice the demigod along the riverside. As the Chief began pulling in the rope, the Wind decided to stay and see what needed to be kept so secret.

What could Sleeping Bear be hiding? It wondered.

Dancing around, it waited until the blanket was removed from the boat, revealing the girl. The Wind, stunned by her beauty, went into a frenzy.

The chief did not know the Wind was paying attention that day. He ignored the blustery afternoon as he gave his daughter food and informed her of the news that came from the tribe.

When his daughter was finished eating, Sleeping Bear helped her back into the canoe, covered her once more, and let the rope out until she was floating in the river.

The Wind was furious. *Why would Sleeping Bear hide away such beauty? She should be seen every day!* Envious of the girl's glamour and enraged at Sleeping Bear for hiding it away, the Wind started up a great gale to blow the cover off the boat. As the Wind swept through, the rope holding the canoe to the tree snapped, too weak to withstand such force. Still, the Wind did not stop. The river's pace quickened as the Wind gusted. Finally, the blanket blew off the canoe and the Wind rejoiced once more at the sight of the girl's beauty.

Sitting up, the Ottawa chief's daughter watched as she floated down the river. Without paddles, there was no way to get back to land. Not knowing the Wind was the culprit of her escape, the girl embraced the breeze that danced along her skin, reminding her how desperately she wanted to be free.

Down the river, the Keeper of the Water Gates stood on the edge of the water looking out over his stead. He was a lonely man with no one to keep him company. While he cherished the river and was proud of his position, he prayed to *Gitchee Manitou* for a wife, someone to help ease his loneliness.

When the Keeper saw the boat coming downriver he rushed out into the water.   Not until he reached the canoe did he see the exquisite girl.   The beauty enraptured the man much like a spell, and he fell instantly under its power.

"The Great Spirit has answered my cry!" He pulled the boat to shore.

The girl was ever grateful to be out of the canoe and no longer rushing down the fierce water.   She smiled at the Keeper and attempted to thank him but he was blinded and deafened by her beauty.

"You will become my wife, the spirits have deemed it so.   I prayed for a wife and here you are, floating down my waters as if a gift for me!"

Setting the canoe on the side of the riverbank, the Keeper brought the girl to his wigwam, abandoning his post early.   The Wind, shocked by the man's selfish nature in taking the girl, became upset with the Keeper.

I set her free and she has been taken, this will not do.

Not wanting to have the girl hidden away, the Wind lashed out at the Keeper.   Gust after gust attacked the man striking him over and over until he fell to the ground, dead.   Once the man's soul rose up to linger with the Wind, it froze.

What have I done?   I killed a man over the girl's beauty just as Sleeping Bear said the mortals would do.

Sagged in grief, the Wind brought the soul to an island in the river, Isle au Peche, and let him free.   *Gitchee Manitou* also felt sorrow for the Keeper, especially because the man thought the girl was a blessing from the Great Spirit.   So, he turned the soul into an oracle to bless the island and all that came to him in meditation and times of need.

The Wind urged the chief's daughter back into the canoe and pushed her upriver to Sleeping Bear, who was grieving along the riverside.

His tears turned to ones of joy when he say his daughter float up in the canoe, safe and sound.

Forgive me, Chief Sleeping Bear, said the Wind.   *I became jealous of your daughter's beauty and accidently sent her boat down the river.   I beg of you, do not cover her beauty, she deserves more.   The Wind wants to dance with her not see her hidden from view.*

"I cannot risk losing my daughter again," the chief said.   "You cannot take her away from me and neither can mortal man.   I fear the suitors who come after my daughter.   War will start over her and I cannot let that happen."

Trying to be helpful, the Wind thought as the chief did.   There had to be a solution.

Finally, one was found.

There is a beautiful island in the river free of man, only decorated with nature.   There she would not be threatened by suitors, but instead unhampered to dance and run and not be hidden away.

Without another option, Sleeping Bear agreed.   Paddling his daughter upriver, he brought her to the island of Wahnabezee.

"You will be safe here, my daughter. *Gitchee Manitou* will see that you are protected from the dangers of this world." Sleeping Bear let his daughter go and watched her walk off into the wilderness.

After the chief floated away and back to his tribe, *Gitchee Manitou* covered the perimeter of the island with snakes, to keep out any mortal tempted to set foot on the land.

The daughter was euphoric, no longer was she forced to hide away but free to explore and run and live life with abandon.

Everything on the island became entranced with the beauty of the demigod's daughter. Even the snakes became enraptured with the girl, and they began to worship her.

When the Great Spirit noticed how the island had fallen under the woman's trance, as well as the Wind, *Gitchee Manitou* blessed the girl with immortality, as long as she stayed on the island. With the gift, the girl was also given the ability to transform into a beautiful doe whenever she desired. A form she would take more often as the Earth changed around her.

While not many who visit Belle Isle come across Chief Sleeping Bear's daughter, a few will catch a glimpse of her either in human or animal form. The blessed will see her, but only a chosen few will be called to run free in the wind with her.

The Cottage

By Edward Ahern

Becky's voice had the nasal rasp of someone who'd been crying. "He's at the cottage now, Fred, but he'll be going into the hospital next week."

It was Tuesday, and I was at an airport waiting for another flight. I heard what Becky didn't say- that this would probably be his last stay outside of a medical facility. I scrounged mentally for a weekend commitment that would prevent me from going, but Uncle Phil was starting to die over a weekend that I had free.

She continued, "Karen's here. I'm going to call Pete next and see if he can come."

Becky and Karen were sisters, mismatched bookends pushed together to hold their father upright. Pete was my brother, who I hadn't talked to since Christmas. Their mother and our mother were sisters.

"I might be able to make it, Becky. I'll call you back and let you know."

"Thanks Fred, I hope you can. It's been two years since you've seen him." Her voice was gentle enough that it almost hid the accusation.

I called my wife, then pocketed the phone and pulled out a note pad.   Getting to Northern Michigan from the east coast was never easy, but there were plenty of open seats to Detroit. I booked flights and a car, then put away the note pad and took my cell phone back out.

Pete's recorded message came on, assuring me that he'd call me right back, which he almost never did. "Pete, it's Fred. Becky just called, Uncle Phil is apparently going downhill. I'm catching a flight to Detroit on Friday, and driving north from there. Let me know if you'd want to drive up with me."

I called Becky back. "Becky? I'll be getting to the cottage Friday evening around six or seven, and leaving Sunday morning. Have you got room to spare, or should I book a motel?"

"That's wonderful, Fred." Her voice sounded clearer. "No, we'll have a room for you. You'll bunk in with Pete if he comes."

Business travelers are stability tested at airport terminals. I shut out the garish posters and videos, the polyglot babbling, the constantly repeated warnings to be suspicious and mistrustful, and hunkered down into remembering.

I'd never stood witness to the death or funeral of a male relative. My father's father had died of cirrhosis in a Chicago hospital. My mother's father had died in a hospital in Tennessee after a car accident. My own father had dropped to the floor of a Texas motel bathroom and died of a heart attack. Our mother had insisted that my brother and I were too young to attend the funerals. Uncle Phil would fit the pattern. If I saw him now I wouldn't be present at his death, and would almost undoubtedly skip his funeral.

My wife and I had agreed that there was no need for her to come-she didn't carry the suitcase memories that would spill open after my arrival. And there seemed to be no reason yet to bother our son with the news. On Friday morning I woke her at 4 a.m. to say goodbye, and she was falling back asleep before I left the bedroom.

LaGuardia to Detroit is almost a shuttle flight. The Detroit airport barricades itself outside the mayhem of the city, and I routed my rental car northwestward to avoid traversing the urban decay. I drove north through Lower Michigan's thumb shape for five hours until I reached the thumbnail.

I'd spent a dozen childhood summers at the cottage, and its lake water and pine wood aroma had permeated me. I slowed down as I reached the last turn.   The approach to the cottage had been a transforming portal, snaking through dense tree stands and over gnarled-root speed bumps to the cottage and the rocky shore of the lake.

But the overgrowth had been thinned and gentrified, and the dirt trails paved over with gravel.   I refused to see what was around me now, holding on to mind pictures of century old trees that grudgingly let me pass in slow, sharp turns, and which in winter died and dropped across the trail to block springtime entry.

The side of the cottage away from the lake and the freestanding garage were still as my mother's father had built them in the early 1930's, but I knew in a quiet hopeless way that the cottage had been wrenched out of the depression and force-fed modernizations.

I walked into the garage, which saggingly clung to its past. The privy was still behind the crudely made wood door inside the back corner of the garage, but the humans and flies and spiders had all abandoned the pit toilet decades ago. There was only the aroma of wet rot.

The well house spring where I'd hand-drunk frigid spring water and stored the perch I'd just cleaned was long gone, buried under an almost suburban lawn. As I walked through the cottage backdoor, still unlocked, I lost my bearings- the mutations making me think I was in a Lake Tahoe time share. What my grandfather had built, constrained by one man's capability, had been work-ganged into spacious conformity.

Becky and Karen, older but archetypically recognizable, met me in the redone living room. They'd already eaten but put together a refrigerator meal for me. Uncle Phil was heavily medicated, and not expected to rouse before morning.

None of us wanted to admit that we were having a rehearsal for a wake, and talked around their sleeping father. Becky started, "Pete got in this morning, but he's gone into town.   You'll be staying with him in the same room you had as kids.   Good trip?"

We had what my mother used to call a good visit, talking of spouses and children and providing sanitized reports of our lives.   We were close enough that the omissions were only occasional.   I felt obliged to testify while the three of us were together.

"You know, our dad died when I was ten and Pete was three.   Your dad always made us welcome, helped out our mom, included us in the holiday dinners..."

Becky interrupted, eyes tearing.   "Thank you so much for coming, you and Pete.   I know what it means to dad."

"I had to come.   Although I do remember what a son-of-a-bitch he was when I crewed for him on the sailboat, and I really remember the times he shanghaied me to shovel dry human manure from the sanitation plant for your garden."

Pete came in while we were still laughing and gave me a quizzical look.

"Just Uncle Phil stories." I hugged him, but he'd swelled since adolescence, so my arms didn't make it all the way around.   We'd lived in the same rooms for thirteen years, and could read each other's moods without talking.   But for over twice that much time we'd lived apart, and now spoke infrequently and met rarely. We were litter mates with the vague sense that we should have kept running together.

Both my cousins looked frayed and blotchy, worn away by caring for the father who'd always sheltered them. Karen spoke up, "We'll all pretty much have to hang out until dad is awake and dressed. The water's not too cold. You could go for a swim tomorrow."

I glanced at Pete, who understood. "We'd better hit the sack. It's been a long day for everybody."

We clambered up the steep, narrow stairs our grandfather had built, and into the cant-ceilinged room where we'd spent most of our summers. The old furniture was gone, reclassified as either show piece antique or junk, but the replacements had the same function-bureau, dresser and wooden bunk bed.

Pete had already commandeered the lower bunk. I fleetingly thought about asserting elder brother privilege, but knew I'd lost any seniority when I'd left home for college and never really returned. My barely teenaged brother had been left to the care of our widowed mother.

I stared for a second at him, wanting to ask what he remembered of our father.   But I already knew the answer-nothing.   Even my memories of our dad were fragmentary.

Banalities were exchanged, and then I asked, "When's the last time you saw Uncle Phil?"

"This afternoon, and maybe two years before that."

"Does he still speak so slowly?"

"Yeah, you'll still want to finish his sentences."

We undressed in silence.   Women make an art of building bridges between themselves with small talk, but I'd been conditioned to approach another man only with purpose in mind.   Pete and I were comfortable in our mutual quiet, but aware that part of our brotherhood was lacking by being unspoken.

Before I climbed the bunk bed ladder, I dropped to all fours and looked under the lower bed.   The enameled bed pan that we'd used as children was still there, but judging by the cobwebs and dead mosquitoes, hadn't been squirted into in years.

Once in bed the stillness of the Michigan night took hold, the only sound the waves lapping in soft hisses over the beach stones.

Stormy or calm, the ebb and surge of the waves had taken over from my childhood heartbeats, rhythmic intervals without measured time, and I'd sleepily hoped that the pulse of my life could continue at that pace.

Breakfast the next morning was disheveled and comfortable, the four of us having spent a decade of summers together at the cottage.   But none of us wanted to speak to the dwindling future asleep in the adjacent room, and talked about the past, all recorded and emotionally safe.

"Karen?   Becky?"

"Dad's awake," the sisters chorused.

Uncle Phil insisted on being dressed and helped out into the front yard facing the lake. He was clearly uncomfortable with his daughters' efforts to make him comfortable, and relieved when he was left with Pete and me.   He spoke more slowly than ever, and I had time between his words to look around the lake.   What had been long stretches of shoreline woods was now a pimpled jaw line of close-set cottages.

"Lot of changes, Uncle Phil."

"The cottage looks good, doesn't it?"

Pete and I exchanged glances.   He spoke first.

"I really like what you've done with the kitchen-it's a lot roomier and more efficient."

My turn, "And the addition to the living room makes it a much better place for entertaining". But I was thinking of my grandmother, who would read her newspaper in the living room stretched out on an army cot next to where the wall had been, and would open up the newspaper sections over her legs and torso so she would stay warm during her nap. I wanted the army cot back.

Uncle Phil asked about my wife and child, and how Pete was surviving down south as a bachelor. His conservative world view was a fortress, but he used our reassurances as mortar for his rampart walls. I thought about hugging him, but knew we would both be uncomfortable.

He faded after a chicken salad lunch that he barely touched, and went back to bed. Pete and I saw him again briefly that evening when he was roused to be given his meds. He was barely articulate, victimized by his illness and his drugs.

We were all up early the next morning, Pete and I because we had to leave, Karen and Becky so they could begin their ministrations. Uncle Phil was awake, laying in the bed my grandfather and grandmother had shared for almost fifty years.

"Uncle Phil, it was great to see you again."

"Glad you could make it up to the cottage. Make sure you get back up here soon."

Men occasionally can achieve intimacy without words, and I held his hand with both of mine. "You take good care of yourself," I said.   His eyes sharpened their focus on me, as if imprinting my image.

Once we left the cottage, Pete and I hugged, the last time we would have contact for months.

I left the radio off during the drive back to the Detroit airport and tried to retrieve memories. I could remember only shards, small moments, a picnic lunch with my uncle's family, a drive in my father's car, and realized that despite our lives together I possessed only incomplete portraits of both men.   Once at the departure gate waiting area I pulled out my phone and called our son.   After his recorded message I left a recording of my own.   "Steve, this is dad.   Hope all is well. Just wanted to let you know that Uncle Pete and I visited Great Uncle Phil.   He's dying, and we went up to say our goodbyes.   I'm sorry that you never really knew him, but I'll try and tell you about him when we get together. Love you."

Harry and Stevie

By James Vescovi

George made me volunteer for a program where you help out old folks, but the guy assigned to me, Harry Jones, died after one visit.

Signing up was the last in a string of punishments George meted out for various "infractions," as he liked to call them. First, he took away my stereo for failing Chemistry and English. After I got three speeding tickets in two weeks, he hacked my curfew down from midnight to 10:00 p.m. Sometime after that, my friend, Chas, got busted by his dad with a bag of pot. When George got wind of it, he didn't believe me when I told him I hadn't smoked any of it.   Since he had nothing left to take away, he added on. He drove me in his sawed-off AMC Gremlin downtown to The Potawatomi, a former Class A hotel turned flophouse for drunks and discharged mental cases.   Behind the front desk, a fat guy pasting S&H Green Stamps in a booklet with a tongue as big as a cow's jerked his thumb at an office door, behind which sat Patti Davis, whose perky tits looked completely out of place in such a dump.   The arched windows in her office hadn't been washed in years, and the smell of stale piss was drifting in from some crack in the wall.   I said I'd come to volunteer for the Senior Services program of Osceola, Michigan, which, judging by the way she scrutinized my Alice Cooper t-shirt and black shoulder-length hair, took her by surprise.   Good thing.   Had I told her I'd been forced to volunteer, she would have sent me packing because, as she repeated three times: "It's so wonderful of you to do this.   I take only enthusiastic people." I had no idea how she could afford to be so choosy.   I didn't see any line of volunteers out the door.   It had to be her first job out of social work school.

I acted gung-ho.   My neighbor, Ted Beane, had done a three-month stint at Senior Services, his sentence for defacing a mural in our high school gymnasium.   With a few strokes of paint, he'd turned our mascot, a Potawatomi brave, into an Injun stoned out of his mind.   Ted was assigned to a good old dude who shared his Tareytons while they watched afternoon movies. Ted's gaffer also showed him World War II photos of his tour in Italy – no combat stuff, but lots of clowning around, drunks on tanks, and a shot-up palace known as the best whorehouse in Sicily.

Patti leafed through a cabinet, pulled a file, and flipped through it.

"I think Harry will be perfect for you," she said.

Harold N. Jones had worked in at a paper mill, a main industry in town. After an on-the-job injury in the 1950s, he hacked a cab, which in Osceola meant you drove fares to the rinky-dink airport, plus an occasional emergency run to the drugstore for an old lady behind on her prednisone. Mr. Jones was sixty-eight, retired, and a widower. His only son had passed away a decade earlier.

Patti's face drew a blank. She mused, "That's strange, his application doesn't list hobbies or special interests."

Did I care? If he liked checkers, we'd play checkers. Maybe Parcheesi was his game. Or we could talk about the good old days when you didn't kiss a girl till the sixth date. All I needed was to show up once a week until George figured I'd done enough time and sprung me.

"And he has no grandchildren," added Patti, befuddled.

What was there to be surprised about? If he had family, he wouldn't have enrolled himself in a program where a teen you didn't know showed up at your home, presumably to keep you company and change a light bulb or two, and could've stolen money you'd left on the dresser or swigged your whiskey when you weren't looking, or worse.

She gave me an index card with Jones's address and phone and instructed me to call on him within a week, but to be sure to telephone first because sometimes the clients got a little confused by it all and refused to open the door to the volunteer.

In ten minutes, it was over: no interview, no background check, no references.

I left the building, where the TV volume from the lounge sounded as if it were coming through a megaphone, and I waited on the stoop for George to finish his errands. The hotel had an Indian motif, with tomahawk door handles and curtains printed with teepees. Two sullen-looking braves held up the portico, with help today from three old boozers leaning against them. It was unbearably hot for May. The men wiped the backs of their hairy necks with handkerchiefs.

They eyed me.   After determining that I was old enough to hit up for a handout, one guy asked me in a raspy voice, "Lend me a quarter for the jug?"

I pulled my pant pocket inside out to show him I was broke, too.   They all nodded and receded back into their conversation, which was about the "lousy prick of a hotel manager" that never came out of his air-conditioned office.   They were still on the subject when George arrived twenty minutes late in the Gremlin.   He'd had it washed and waxed but it remained the ridiculous car it was.

Harry Jones resided at 17 Betancourt, Apartment 78.   I had to look up the address on a map, despite the fact that I'd not only lived in this town my entire life, but also my friends and I were always scouting obscure neighborhoods to find liquor stores that would sell us Stroh's or Mateus.   Locating Betancourt was like being in a familiar park and coming upon on a pond you never knew existed.

Except Betancourt was no pond.   It was lined with vacant lots and defunct tool and dye shops.   Number 17, a rectangular tower made of bricks the color of potato skins, shot up from a dustbowl of a parking lot.   Soaring off the roof was a blackened smokestack held in place by guy wires.   The apartments had sliding windows over baby blue panels.   There were more cigarette butts in the shrub beds than weeds.

The lobby door was supposed to be secured, but the lock didn't catch.   Still, I rang old Jones from the house phone to let him know I was coming up.   It took five minutes to explain who I was, despite the fact we'd spoken the evening before.   He didn't sound suspicious – just dumb.   Or maybe he'd gotten cold feet about allowing a stranger into his home.   He hemmed and hawed, trying to make a decision, until I suppose he threw the dice and said to himself, "To hell with it.   I'll take my chances," and told me to come on up.

The hallway on his floor was dank and dimly lit.   I rang his doorbell, which produced a lively BING-BONG tone like one belonging to a colonial in one of Osceola's choosy neighborhoods.   Jones took a long time to get to the damn door and opened it without looking through the peephole because he had cataracts.   This is why he'd signed up at Senior Services.

"Can't see good anymore and don't want to have the damn surgery, either!" he said, showing me into his kitchen.   It was small, with painted-over cabinet glass and a crowded fly strip hanging from the ceiling. On the table was a Lazy Susan holding salt substitute and pepper, plastic container labeled "Chow Chow," and a jar of Marshmallow Fluff.

The kitchen got quiet after Harry shut off a fan that was doing a bad job of ridding the air of a greasy odor.   He invited me to sit. The chairs had cushions, though he hadn't bothered to tie them on.

Before I could make him and myself feel more comfortable by saying what a nice place he had, he launched into a long complaint about barely getting by on his pension and about living in such a building and "the situation with all kinds of undesirables, colored, Mexicanos, white, you name it"—I think to let me know that if I was going to rip him off I'd be disappointed with the haul.

I accepted his offer of a can of soda. He got a Diet Fresca from under the sink and served it with ice in a plastic cup whose sides were as clawed up as the lenses on his glasses. I hated diet soda, but drank it anyway.   A guy as skinny as Harry had no reason to drink the stuff and probably put it in the shopping cart out of habit because he used to buy it for a fat wife.

In addition to the kitchen, the apartment had a bedroom, whose door was closed, and a living room, where Jones invited me to bring my drink and watch TV.   He pointed me to a couch covered with a wool blanket that looked as if a dozen kittens had had their way with it. He lowered himself into a La-Z-Boy, which I could tell from a mile away was where he wiled away his hours.

"You like game shows?" he hollered above the volume.

I nodded, though I wondered what he could possibly see through those glasses, covered with fingerprints and crud.

After a while, I got claustrophobic sitting in this dingy place and watching housewives win washer/dryers. If Harry wasn't going to tell me any World War II stories, or talk about a famous passenger he'd picked up in his cab – and judging by his bare walls he didn't seem like the type of guy who wanted to recall the past – I wanted to do whatever chores he had for me and get out.

At the next commercial break, I told him, "I'm not allowed to watch TV on school days."

After a long pause, he observed, "That's good."

He turned his gaze back to the TV. With his long index finger, he nervously tapped the arm of his chair.

"Do you need any shopping done?" I asked to prod him along.

"Well, I don't really require anything today," he replied.

Harry was a little over six feet tall. He was wide at the hips, with a bald head that looked like half an eggshell. He had a long neck and a bobbing Adam's apple. Under his leathery skin, it looked like a prune was lodged in his throat. His long fingernails were blackened with soot, and he wore sky blue slacks and a dress shirt buttoned up to his razor-scraped neck.

The apartment, with its low, water-stained ceiling, really oppressed me. I informed him, well above the TV volume, "I can only come once a week, so maybe you'll want to check on your supplies."

That comment made him slump in his La-Z-Boy. He got an angry look on his face and started scraping his upper lip with his teeth. He jumped up and went to the kitchen. I followed him.

He opened a cupboard door and pushed a few cans around to make it sound fully stocked up.

"Nah, I don't need nothing," he said.

I couldn't return to Dick Clark and "The $10,000 Pyramid."

"Maybe some soup or milk for your coffee?" I asked.

"I use CoffeeMate," he said.

"What about bread?   You got a loaf stored in the freezer?   Bread goes bad fast in this heat.   Or how about watermelon?   It's good for you.   Keeps you hydrated."

He looked at me, dumbfounded as to how a youngster possessed this housewifely knowledge that he'd gained only after his wife had passed on.

"Well, guess I could use a few things," he sighed.

He rummaged through a counter drawer for something to write with, and we sat down at the table again.   Harry licked the tip of the pencil, which I'd seen my grandfather do and never asked why, and put on his thinking cap.   It took him ten seconds to conjure up each item.   His block-like, jumbled handwriting reminded me of the ransom note whose letters were cut from magazines that was shown on TV when Patty Hearst was kidnapped.

Finally, he dug into his pocket, removed a bill, and held it a few inches from his eyes. When he saw it was $1, he placed his hands on the table, like a man who'd just received bad news.

Now he had a logistical problem: How was he going to fetch more money without me seeing where he hid it?

I decided to help him out because I had to get out of there. "Do you mind if I use your bathroom?" I asked.

It didn't seem to relieve him.

His face lit up. "Hand me that, will you?" he asked, pointing over my shoulder at a pink canister marked "BISCUIT FLOUR."

He popped open the lid. "Lookee here, keep a few greenbacks here for a rainy day," he said, pulling out some fives. He handed me the shopping list and the bills, which were so worn they felt like flower petals.

"I'll be back in a half hour," I said.

As he followed me to the door, he asked, "What'd you say your name was?"

I hadn't said because when I entered his apartment he hadn't noticed my extended hand.

"Steve," I replied.

"Okay, Steve. You know where the market is?"

There was one down the street near where I'd gotten off the bus.

"Langenhort's, right?"

"That's the one," he said.

He shot me a wave and closed the door, with a look of relief that suggested he knew he'd never see me again, but twenty dollars was a small price to pay for a visit he'd been damn foolish to set up in the first place.

I left the building and threaded my way through the parking lot, whose cracked asphalt held scattered battered luxury cars with peeling landau roofs and Japanese compacts. The air was filling with humidity. I guessed that Harry was looking down on me from his seventh-floor window. I thought about easing his anxiety by turning around and waving, but said to hell with it. He'd probably given up on me and was back in the La-Z-Boy watching "Joker's Wild."

Langenhort's was a local chain where my mother shopped, but our location was nothing like the one on Betancourt. It was dirty and decrepit. The cashiers were not bubbly teenagers. They were middle-aged, overweight black women and young, gaunt white guys who looked strung out on drugs and despair. The groceries reflected the lower economic level of the neighborhood: lots of junk food; pigs knuckles in the meat section; generic Rice Krispies; canned chop suey; and a produce section without a single customer in it.   I grabbed a cart and soon located everything on Harry's list: canned pinto beans; a family-size package of chicken wings; Fresca; pork rinds; pickles; Sanka; ice milk; and watermelon, which I wondered whether he added on my account.

Approaching the checkout lanes, I locked eyes with a cashier.   We both looked away.   Most people would've gone to another lane, but I had to get a closer look at this guy. He was in his mid-twenties, with watery eyes, and his cheeks and forehead were scarred by acne.   He had short blond hair parted straight down the middle and a nervous habit of combing it with his fingers.

He made no greeting, though it didn't strike me as rudeness.   He was probably pre-occupied, thinking, "He doesn't belong in this neighborhood," while I was thinking, "I wonder if seeing downtrodden guys like this and Harry are what George wanted me to get out of this experience?"

Then I decided, "The guy must be a fag. That's why he's got a shell-shocked look and works in a dump like this, because the management at Sears Roebuck or at the Osceola Savings & Loan won't hire him. That's why he's employed on Betancourt."

With thin, veiny hands, Roger – the name on a tag pinned to his white shirt – rang me up. We had a tense moment when I held out my money just as he turned to bag the groceries. He looked like a deer caught in headlights, and I thought, "Shit, this guy is fragile."

I suppose being taught to defer to customers, he released the brown paper bag and took my bills, which, for some reason, I was glad were not new and crisp. After giving me change, he bagged me up with great care, moving items from one bag to another, as if this task was the only one in the job he could take pride in.

I picked up my bags and thanked him, though he didn't acknowledge it, and headed back to Jones's. A breeze had blown up. From a distance, I could see curtains of all colors – blue, pink, beige – dancing in the windows of 17 Betancourt. You'd think the motion would lighten the building's mood, but the feeling was one of disuse, as if the residents had fled with their windows open.

There were more cars in the parking lot now, presumably those of people returning home from work. The sight really weighed on me: rows of junkers with inane bumper stickers and children's clothing scattered on the rear dash, here and there a tailgate left ajar. I went up in the elevator with a guy in dirty overalls who I suspected might have given me a hassle had his eyes not been clouded over by his own troubles.

I rang Harry's bell. The volume on the TV went down, and I heard the shuffling of Harry's slippers on the floor. It was too painful for me to make him go through the suspense of wondering who it was, so I called out, "It's me, Steve. With your groceries."

The door opened. His eyes widened behind his lenses.

"Hello, Stevie!" he said, with a big smile.

I entered and set the bags on the kitchen table.

"Got everything," I said, holding up the list.

I took his hand and plopped the change into it. He picked up a magnifying glass and passed it up and down the receipt, moving his lips as he tallied things up.

He poked his head into a bag and began emptying it like a child with a Christmas stocking.

"Well, lookee here!" he said, holding up a package of glazed windmill cookies.

"These are my favorites, yes sir," he chirped, as he muscled the chicken wings out.

"I've been a-hankering for this," he announced, holding the block of chocolate ice milk.

Jones's apartment, which faced west, was hotter than ever. His delight was driving me nuts. I couldn't wait for a commentary on each item.

"I've just looked at the clock, Mr. Jones, and I think I should be going."

He froze.

"Really?" he asked, in a near giddy voice, as if now assured that this young punk with hair like a girl's had come simply to perform the deed that the lady at Senior Services said he would. "Don't want some ice milk?" he asked.

That slashed my heart a bit. As a child, I spent summers at the lake house of my grandmother, a real snob who'd inherited lots of money from her father. When we shopped at the general store, she snickered at the ice milk, a cheaper version of ice *cream*, as if people who bought it were among P. T. Barnum's biggest suckers.

"No, thanks," I replied. "I have to get home for supper."

"Well, suit yourself, then." Harry wasn't going to push his luck.

I followed him to the front door and stepped into the hallway.

"You call me Harry from now on," he stated. "Right, Stevie?"

"Okay. See you, Harry. See you next week."

He raised a hand, as if there was no need for such a declaration because now he knew I was a decent fellow. What luck! He calmly closed the door.

As I waited for the elevator, I heard him whistle. For a guy like Harry, the tune sounded surprisingly lively – even rambunctious.

I didn't want to wait at the bus shelter facing the Langenhort family's black-sheep-of-a-supermarket. Instead, I walked ten minutes to a stop in the center of town. Across the street, the usual moochers loitered around the entrance of The Potawatomi.

When I got home, I was relieved to find that my parents were out for the evening, and I wouldn't have to give them a report of my mercy mission. I shot baskets in the driveway until it got dark, ate some peanut butter and jelly sandwiches, and went to bed.

Patti called the following day to see how things went.

"Fine," I said, stingy with my words.

When she phoned three days later, telling me that Harry had gotten dizzy, fallen and been hospitalized, I was shocked. At first, I thought she was going to tie me into it. But then she told me that, after a bunch of tests, the doctors had diagnosed an inoperable tumor. I couldn't think of anything to say and, after a long silence, she attempted to comfort me as if I were a boy who'd lost a pet. She then informed me that, under Senior Services rules, I was under no obligation to visit Harry at the hospital, but "it might be nice." To this I also said nothing.

She offered to find a new codger for me, but I said I'd really hit it off with Harry and was feeling very low right now and needed to wait awhile before calling on anyone new. She seemed surprised at the depth of my feeling for the old man, but told me that "getting back into the water" with another client was the best way of getting over my sorrow.

I hung up and raised my fist in the air! George would never know about this. Now I could fake my visits and use the time to hit record stores and head shops downtown. With luck, the deceit would last long enough for George to be satisfied and let me off.

But that didn't mean I didn't visit Harry. Later that day, I rode the bus to the hospital and was directed to his room.   The bed by the door was empty.   I heard the suction in tubes and beeping machines even before I parted the curtain of the other bed.   It was depressing, but, I thought, at least he wasn't getting stiffed on medical care because he wasn't rich and didn't look it.

I studied him.   Harry was out cold.   It looked too deep for normal sleep.

I nearly jumped when I saw a girl on the opposite side of the bed, with her back toward me, looking out the window.   Her brown hair was silky, all the way down to her leather belt. She had a full round ass, and distribution of flesh on her back and arms suggested she had a great pair of knockers.

Harry smacked his dry mouth.   He looked awful, his eyes wrenched closed as if he were seconds away from a head-on collision. His wrinkles didn't make him look wise, like they do with some old people.   They were etched indifferently on his face.   They made him appear seedy.   On the night table sat his glasses--of no use to him nor good enough for the Goodwill Store after he passed.   His stomach was sunken, and I thought about all that crappy food he ate.   Maybe his wife had been a good cook.   I got angry that he didn't at least have a photo of her near his La-Z-Boy.

Maybe it was in his bedroom. It struck me how pathetic it was that after I turned up with his groceries, he made out like I was a good friend of his now. He'd offered a bowl of chocolate ice milk to seal our compact.

The girl picked up a can of Tab on the window ledge. I studied her, wondering if I'd seen her around town or at a school dance. I couldn't wrap my head around the fact that she and Harry were in the same room. Had he known her?   Or was she another of Patti's Good Samaritans?   There was something about her presence that made me mad. I'd been hoping to say something decent to Harry, but not with anyone around. At the same time I didn't want to pass up any opening with her.

She wore an MIA bracelet. They were all the rage among high school girls. It gave them a chance to fantasize that the heroic soldier was their lover, pining away for them in a jungle prison. It never occurred to them that, were the guy ever to make it out of a POW camp, he'd hardly be a candidate for normal marriage. He'd wake up screaming at night or shoot up his place of business after they'd fired him.

"Yoo-hoo, I'm here. . ." a voice sang out.

I turned around to see a woman my mother's age, standing in the doorway.

"Time to go, honey," the woman said.

The girl reached for her leather handbag and slung it over her shoulder. Her face was beautiful, round cheeks but not jowly, and full curvy lips. She brushed a strand of hair behind an ear, smiled at me.

"Did you say your farewells to Harry?" the woman asked.

"Yes," the girl replied curtly.

She was gone. Had she not left her Tab can on the ledge, I would've been certain I was dreaming.

I went around to the other side of Harry's bed and cleared my throat. Just then, a nurse came in and announced the end of visiting hours. Without looking at me, she smoothed out Harry's blanket and said, "We're just keeping him comfortable."

I'd seen enough TV to know what that meant.

I didn't visit Harry again, but kept calling the hospital. When they no longer listed him as a patient, I looked for a death notice in the newspaper. It appeared with the name of the funeral home where he was to be waked.

My mother, who had an errand to run downtown, saved me from the interminable bus trip by driving me to Harry's. She knew nothing about his death. After turning on Betancourt, we passed a tavern that catered to Mexicans. They materialized every summer to pick berries and peaches outside of town.

We pulled up to a stop sign. Under the word STOP, someone had painted ALL HONKEYS. My mother turned to me and smiled, as if she could appreciate the impulse of the oppressed to mar signage. To George it would've been vandalism, pure and simple.

"I didn't know they had a location down here," my mother observed, as we passed Langenhort's.

As we rolled into Harry's lot, she said, "I'd almost like to come with you."

She often made these comments. They came out of nowhere and made you think she was either an angel or the flakiest human alive.

"What are you talking about?" I asked, irritably. What I meant was both, "Why don't you get lost and leave me to my misery?" or "Why the hell would you want to risk parking a shiny 1975 Buick Regal in this scummy neighborhood?"

"I'd like to watch you, in action," she added, "like a fly on the wall."

I'd reported nothing to my parents about liking Harry.   I wouldn't have given them the satisfaction.   Like every adult in my life, she wanted to see me do good.

"Is he a kind man?" she asked.

"What does it matter?   I've got to help him and that's that," I replied, throwing open the car door.

"You'll take the bus home?"

"Yes." I slammed the door shut with my sneaker and walked into the building.   She drove off while I pretended to call Harry on the house phone.

I had a few hours to kill before the wake.   There was no place to go and I didn't want to kick around downtown, afraid my mother would see me.   I went up to Harry's apartment.

A rogue thought hit me: If Harry'd been rushed out by ambulance, chances are his door was unlocked.   He was the kind of old-timer who stashed money all over the house. Imagine the pay-off! And he was dead.   It wasn't like I was robbing him.   I pictured his ecstatic face when I returned with his groceries: Wouldn't he want me to reward myself for the last act of kindness anyone ever did him?

As I'd suspected, the door was open. The carpet was littered with plastic packaging from a syringe and other stuff the paramedics had left behind. A pair of old patched gray pants lay inside-out across the back of a chair. The sight of it all made me feel bad for the old guy and killed my appetite for stealing. Instead I sat in his chair, and watched "Jokers Wild" for a while, but my curiosity about Harry was getting the best of me. I had this urge, I don't know where it came from, to know something about him--something above the dumbass facts I'd gotten from Patti. I began opening drawers—nothing out of the ordinary: pads of paper, stamps, rusty scissors. Another cabinet contained boxes of unused Christmas cards and a broken radio. Harry seemed so bland.

"C'mon, Harry," I said aloud. "You must have a few dark secrets – maybe a few porn movies stashed somewhere?" I laughed. "Were you a closet Nazi? Where's your Storm-Trooper uniform hidden?"

Then I stopped. What I was doing didn't seem right. I didn't know Harry well enough to go randomly snooping. I sat down again, but not in his La-Z-Boy. In the apartment next door something substantial crashed—something on par with a fruit bowl or champagne bottle.   Two men with very squeaky voices started arguing, on and on and on.   I could make out their words.   Like most drunks, they were fighting over nothing—the inane.

"Shut the fuck up!" I yelled. "Motherfuckers! Or I'm going to blow my top!"

Their apartment went dead silent.

I fell in the couch, laughing at the thought of them thinking it was mild old Harry who'd blown his gasket.

But I had something important to do.   I couldn't stand the idea of Harry being abandoned by the world and set out to look for evidence that at least one person gave a damn.   I began poking around again.   Jesus, there had to be a photo of his wife.   I went to the bedroom.   One dresser that was his wife's had a lot of perfume bottles; on top of the other was a phonograph.   An orange bedspread sat crookedly on the Queen-size.   I pictured Harry doing that on the day he'd collapsed.   What a waste of time.

No photos on the dresser or walls, so I began opening drawers.   All I found were white socks, v-neck sweaters, and handkerchiefs.   A small box on his dresser contained tie clips, a special license from 1962 to hunt moose, and a NIXON/AGNEW campaign button.

I went to his night table and open a drawer. Inside was a sawed off baseball bat, I would guess for unwelcome visitors, and a disused-looking box of Trojans.

I went to the kitchen and sat at the table. The cabinet magnets didn't work, and the doors hung open, revealing nothing but cans of Harry's lousy food, glassware, and statuettes of ducks and horses, which had to be his wife's.

A clock above the sink hummed. Soiled hot pads hung from hooks near the stove. I gave the Lazy Susan a spin, wondering, "Is this how Harry lived? In this stupid silence, with nothing on the walls?" Had neighbors even ever seen him? And who the hell was that bodacious girl with her back to his hospital bed?

Around six, I hoofed it to the funeral home. A guy in a dark suit at the front desk directed me to a room packed with people. I thought he'd sent me to the wrong wake until, through the crowd, I caught a glimpse of Harry. Laid out in a navy blue blazer with gold buttons and a yellow lapel handkerchief, he looked like a naval officer, about to be buried at sea. He was framed by flower arrangements. The casket looked fancier than the cheap pine box I expected he'd spend eternity in.

I waited before paying my respects, afraid people would ask me what relation I was. I planted myself on a folding chair against a wall next to two women who prattled on about everything except Harry.

"So where's Michael?" asked one, wearing eye shadow as thick as war paint.

"At Little League," the other replied. "It's a championship game. Lew and I talked about it, but we decided, Harry would have wanted him to play."

Mourners at my rich grandmother's wake spoke in low voices and stood before her shriveled up body with reverence. It was as if they were afraid she'd sit up in the casket and scold them for bad etiquette.

Harry's visitation was more like a spontaneous get-together. People, who I suppose hadn't seen each other in years, laughed and slapped each other on the back. Across the room a guy with a soot black goatee, a bolo, and cowboy boots was holding a lit cigarette out a window. He was the only person besides Harry who was decently dressed. Everyone else looked like the wake was one stop on Saturday morning errands. I didn't know exactly why I'd come, and my clothing showed my vacillation: a corduroy sport jacket; decent slacks, but not the best in my closet; a pair of scuffed up dress shoes.

Like I said, I didn't want to call attention to myself.

The Little League moms dashed off.   I pictured little Michael playing outfield under a soft evening sky.   Was Harry's view of himself so insignificant that he wouldn't have objected to the kid skipping his wake?

A year earlier, a guy at my high school flipped his red Pontiac Bonneville on an icy road at eighty miles per hour and killed himself.   It had been almost impossible to I.D. him.   His name was Eddie DeAngelo, a chunky guy with a mop of black hair.   People liked him because he made fun of his Dago roots. Everyone in school showed up for his wake. The funeral home was so jammed that the condolence line ran down the block.   The principal had to be called, along with the police, because kids were going outside to drink beer or smoke weed in the parking lot.

Eddie wasn't a close friend of mine.   I didn't want to go, but when a friend called me and told about the huge crowd, I drove over. I got there fifteen minutes before the wake ended, paid my respects at the closed casket, and went from group to group, looking for a familiar face.   Actually, I was listening for final words about Eddie, except no one was saying anything about him.   There were mostly arguments about where to get drunk or stoned in his honor.   In fifteen minutes—the time it took to eat lunch with Eddie in the cafeteria while he cracked stale Mafia jokes— and he'd be gone from us forever. I left. I couldn't stand around while the poor bastard's final minutes ticked away. The sensation was familiar at Harry's wake, but I stuck around.

A woman with a white pocketbook the size of a gym bag thumped down next to me. She surveyed the room with a defensive look. Like me, she seemed alienated from the crowd. I was so disgusted by the disregard for Harry that I decided to vent, hoping she was a kindred spirit.

"What a herd," I said.

"I'm surprised," she said. "I didn't expect so many people."

"Did Harry have a big family?" I asked.

"All dead. Two sisters and a brother. And his late son."

I gestured at a tall man who seemed to be acting as host.

"Who's that?"

The woman unbuttoned a black coat, but didn't take it off. "His nephew, Dale."

I said to the woman, "If you want to go say hello to Harry, don't let me stop you."

"They aren't interested in me," she replied with a scowl. "They wouldn't know what to say to me."

"Same here," I said.

"How did you know him?"

"It's not worth talking about," I replied.

"Why wouldn't I want to hear about it?" she asked in her defensive tone.

After a long pause, I said, "I was a Senior Services volunteer. I helped Harry out...."

"How sweet of you..."

"...once."

She gave me a look of uncertainty.

"Then he died," I added.

"You only got to visit him once?"

I nodded.

"What a shame for Harry—and for you," she said.

"I just started. I went to the hospital, too, but he was gone by then – not able to recognize anyone."

"Oh, the hospital," she said, pinning a cobalt blue pocketbook to her hefty bosom. "The nurses treated him awfully. I used to be an LPN. I know these things.

"He was the scapegoat patient for the week," she continued. "I don't know why it is, but nurses always have to have one patient on the floor who's the butt of jokes. I've always figured it's due to the stress of caring, the pressure."

What the hell was there to say to that? She seemed a little "off" to me.

"But at a Catholic hospital? " she went on. "You'd expect better. Nurses are fine women, don't get me wrong, but they get a mob mentality."

She turned to face me for the first time. "I'm Josie," she said. She did not extend her hand. She seemed not so interested in me as in presenting herself. She wore heavy blue eye shadow that made her eyes look as if emerging from a cold pool.

"Well, don't you want to know what they did to him? The answer is nothing. Zip. No compassion. Didn't smile. Made him feel like he was part of the mattress if he could've felt anything."

Dale, the nephew, was asking guests to take their seats.

"Do you want to know who I am?" the woman whispered. One of her front teeth was thinly lined with crimson lipstick. "I'm an old girlfriend. Can you believe I was once pretty enough to be a girlfriend? Harry and I dated after high school. He didn't want to get married, not for a while. But I stuck with him. Did you know Harry was an aspiring songwriter?"

Before I could answer, she said, "That's a silly question. You met him once, and he didn't tell people, anyway. He lettered in track, too. He was a high jumper."

I was too stupefied by the image of Harry's frail body arcing over a pole higher than he was tall to react.

"He wrote songs. Rock'n'Roll, but the old stuff," she went on, "in the way of the Orioles, the Chordettes. Or Bill Hayley. He always kept a little notepad in his pocket for lyrics that came to him. He was never much of a musician, but he knew how to put words and music together. He liked the teens' music, he really did. He sent away hundreds of songs. It's what was near and dear to him in life."

"Somehow, I can't picture Harry as a songwriter."

"What's so wrong with it?" she asked indignantly.

I didn't want to cross her.   I replied, "I don't know.   I guess it's just my narrow view of what a song writer might look like."

"He had talent, believe me," she said, glaring across the room.   "But it didn't amount to much.   He got some interest from Los Angeles, but nothing came through.   He bided his time writing ad jingles for car dealerships.   One time he sold one to a hotel in Chicago, a really beautiful place, marble lobby, where big shots stayed.   He was so excited.   He said, 'Josie, it's been a long time in coming, but this could be it – the mustard seed that is going to sprout and then grow into something big and good.'

"At the end of the day, he got no mustard, no hotdog, nothing," she said with a sigh.   "Soon after, he broke it off with me. Just like that.   Harry was the superstitious type.   He associated me with his bad luck.   It hit me like a freight car.   I thought he was too smart for that.

"A couple of years later, he married Adele, who was also in our high school, but two years younger than me," Josie went on. "After I heard she died, I called him.   I was divorced by then, no children.   He didn't even want to get together for a cup of coffee.   We could've been great friends."

The room had quieted down, and Dale, standing before a podium, thanked everyone for coming. Josie leaned over and whispered, "He's the executor," while fanning herself with a funeral home brochure.

"No priest or minister...wasn't Harry's cup of tea," she whispered.

Dale must've held some kind of sales job, because he seemed comfortable speaking in front of people, though he wasn't as captivating as he thought he was. And he didn't say much about Harry beyond what I knew from Senior Services. He tossed out some platitudes that were so general that the deceased couldn't been anyone. It was like a justice of the peace marrying two people he'd met two minutes earlier.

The worst was the closing words. Even though he hadn't made a single connection between Harry and anything French, he placed his hand on the casket and said, *Au revoir,* Harry."

People lightly applauded when he left the podium. Even by my standards, it was crass.

Everyone began gathering up their belongings. I sank in my chair.

"I don't get it," I said to Josie. "Who are all these people? When I went to his apartment, it was a pigsty – I mean, no one seemed to be taking care of him.   He had to send for someone like me."

Josie's cheeks reddened, though she didn't reply.

Then the logic of it jumped out at me: the big turnout, the girl at the hospital.

"Oh, I get it!" I said.   "He's got money, right?   He sold a bunch of his songs to big pop stars and never told anyone, and now his relatives are expecting to find out he was a millionaire or something."

"Harry wasn't that secretive," Josie replied, staring glumly at me.   "With him, what you saw was what you got."

She turned up the collar of her coat and said, "It's nice to have met you."

She removed a prescription bottle from her purse and tapped a blue pill into her palm.

"Was there water fountain on the way in?" she asked.

"It's off the lobby by the restrooms," I said.

"You're a good young man."

"No.   I'm not."

"Don't be silly." She stood up.   "Harry would not have held a grudge against them."

She joined the crowd shuffling out the door—but hesitantly, like a driver easing her way into a bottleneck without getting her car scratched.

If you ask me, there was urgency in everyone's steps, to scram before they realized that attending his wake, as a form of penance, was a shit-poor gesture. I wondered how long the old man had gone, waiting around for someone to step in and help him out, before he called Senior Services.

While paying for his groceries, I'd found Harry's expired taxi license stuck between bills. He had on those stupid, horned-rim glasses that inflated his eyes.   On his head was a typical woolen hacker's cap.   He wore a mischievous smile that stretched from cheek to cheek, almost as if drawn by a cartoonist.

It made me think Harry was a fun guy to ride with.   Maybe he talked about his attempt at songwriting or just shot the breeze. Above all, he looked like the kind of guy who, had he passed a wino stumbling along the sidewalk, would've given him a free lift to The Potawatomi.

This bunch of relatives and friends or whoever they were struck me as people who would've called Harry for a cab ride and expected it comped.   Had he made big money off his songs, they would have sponged off him.   But they would've done it in small amounts.   They were nickel and dimers, people of no vision.

Not that I had anything to brag about. After my first visit, I'd been dreaming up ways to speed up my routine to get out of his apartment faster.   Had there been a second, he would've invited me to join him in a bowl of ice milk.   I'd have begged off.

The room had emptied out.   An undertaker cleared his throat.   I looked up. Standing next to him was George.   He was looking in my direction but behind me at Harry's casket.   He turned and went out. When he drove me home, he said Patti had called the house that afternoon with the name of another charity case because Harry had died.   I'd become Samaritan to an old maid schoolteacher of eighty-eight.

But for now, I was the last guest.   I hadn't paid respects to Harry, but didn't think it was right to be the final one to kneel at his casket, so I said my good-byes from where I was.

The funeral home had laid Harry out without his glasses.   No wonder: The scummy lenses would have reminded visitors of neglect.   I wish I'd told some of them about

Harry's hesitation while talking to me on the lobby phone, debating with himself whether I was a punk who'd break his skull and rob him—no rare occurrence among the elderly on Betancourt. When he got his groceries, he gave me such an elated look—his appreciation was really over the top. Maybe his ex-girlfriend was right. Either he couldn't see our sins from behind his glasses or simply chose to ignore them.

Off the Bluff of

Big Bay

By Catlin Siem

Standing tall above Superior

sits brick red as flame.

Atop the jagged rock

a lonely wife proclaims,

"Keeper of the Light has gone

astray.   I am not to blame."

The car puttered over the dirt road. While the speed was slow enough to be surpassed by horse and buggy, the passengers did not complain. Riding in an automobile was thrilling no matter the speed.

Clara's giggles from the front seat floated around the car before traveling out the open windows and getting lost in the twilight sky. Helen did her best to ignore the couple sitting in front of her. They were being cute, complimenting each other before bickering about miniscule things just so they could kiss and make up again, and Helen found it a bit too much for her taste. It made the hour drive feel longer. But she reminded herself that once they reached her Walter, she would be the same way. So she left the lovebirds alone.

This was the first time Helen was able to visit Walter at the lighthouse since his promotion to Keeper of the Light there. Why he would desire to be a lighthouse keeper was beyond her, and was the root of their last fight before his departure. Letters were exchanged and apologies made but she hoped spending a night wrapped in his arms would ease her misgivings.

Light cut through the trees ahead of the car, piercing the deep purples and blues of the sky above them. With a flash, the light disappeared only to break through the treetops once more. The road opened up into flat grass in front of the lighthouse. The headlights broke through the twilight and showed dark red brick on the building. The light atop the building swept high into the sky and flashed its beam of light in a steady pattern that seemed to help calm Helen's nerves.

A door opened, spilling light out to meet the headlights, and framed a man in silhouette. He was tall, comfortably filling the doorway. His slightly bowed legs and hands settled in his pockets gave him away.

The smile of recognition never left Helen's soft face as she anxiously waited for the car to stop. The man in the door stayed put until the visitors parked and crawled out of the brand new automobile. Once Helen's feet touched the ground she ran for Walter. The straight-line dress she wore restricted her legs forcing her to shorten her stride.

Her boyfriend walked down the steps and toward her until they met in between the glowing lights of the building and car. Throwing her arms around him, Helen squealed with delight as Walter wrapped his arms around her slim waist and spun her in a circle.

Their lips came together in a kiss that was long overdue. Excitement surged through

Helen as any doubts vanished and she was only left with the thrill of being in Walter's arms. When he sat Helen back on the ground he looked over her shoulder at his friend.

"Frederick!" Walking past Helen, Walter strode up to his friend. They hugged quickly before stepping away. "What's this?" He asked, clapping a hand on Frederick's shoulder. They turned to stare at the dark blue automobile.

"A 1911 Ford Model T Touring." Helen was certain she could see Frederick's chest puff up from where she stood. "Straight off the line. Father received it last month. I finally convinced him to let me take Clara out for a drive the other day. That went smoothly so he allowed me the car again tonight."

Helen walked over to the other girl and watched the boys talk. Caught between the car's headlights and the light still pouring from the door, Frederick and Walter were lit up and glowing as brightly as the lighthouse light above them. Walter's vivid red hair was longer than Helen had ever seen it before, curling down around his ears and across his forehead. Being full of excitement earlier she hadn't noticed and now she couldn't seem to get over how unruly he looked next to Frederick, whose hair was short, dark, and sleek. His hair matched his attire, the gray riding coat still fastened closed and his matching trousers were in perfect order. Walter was also in trousers but they were not pressed nor the current style, and he wore only an undershirt.

Even though he looked disheveled and out of sorts compared to the crispness of Frederick, there was something about Walter that still made Helen swoon.   He was a hardworking man who was on his own while all of their friends still lived at home.   Pride surged through Helen's chest.

"Come on, this is one of the calmest nights I've seen since coming up here," Walter said after he and Frederick were done discussing the car.   "There's a firepit on the west side of the building.   How about we get a fire going and enjoy the night?"

The visitors agreed and, after Frederick turned the car's lights off, they headed toward the brick building.

Walter came up beside Helen and wrapped his arm around her shoulders.   "It's so good to see you, have I mentioned this yet?"

A smile grew on her rouge lips.   "You have not."

"You're more beautiful than in my dreams. If that is even possible, especially in that dress."

Blush decorated Helen's cheeks.   The dress she wore was new and while she wouldn't admit to purchasing the dress just for this occasion, she was pleased that he seemed to notice.

"You dream about me?"

"Oh, every night.   But lucky for me, I won't have to worry about seeing you only in my dreams tonight." Walter bent down and planted a kiss on his girlfriend's cheek.   "My thoughts are, we enjoy the fire for a little while and then when Frederick and Clara are distracted with each other, we can sneak off for a bit, spend some time running around with only the flash of the lighthouse beacon as our guide."

Helen's cheeks were so hot from her blush that it felt like they might catch fire.   Walter was much more forthright than usual, something must have changed him while working at the lighthouse.   But as embarrassed as she felt at the comment, Helen was thrilled at the thought of running around at night with her love.

When the fire was lit, the couples sat down on worn blankets on either side of the fire, only catching glimpses of the other when the fire crackled low before rising up again.

"I am so glad you were able to visit me," Walter said.   Helen sat in between his legs with Walter's arms wrapped around her. "I get along with the assistant well enough, however he is not always the best company as he spends his free time with his wife and children more often than not."

"Where are they?" Helen asked. No one had made an appearance since they arrived.

"On their side of the lighthouse. It is broken into two homes, mine is this side, his the other."

"Clara almost didn't make it out with us," Frederick said from behind the flames. Helen forgot the other two were there, the conversation felt interrupted now.

"Father was the one who discovered the old lighthouse keeper's body. He was very adamant that we shouldn't come up here when he heard where we were going. You'd think he wouldn't be so uneasy about the area anymore, it has been almost ten years."

"William Prior was his name," Walter said. "I read all about him in the logbook when I started working here. His wife and children waited and searched for him for four months before they moved to Marquette. William wasn't found until a year after that, and there was no proof of whether he hung himself or was murdered. He's a bit of a legend here already. My assistant's children have claimed his ghost is here and have seen him more than once. I haven't seen the ghost myself, but I have heard more than my fair share of doors shut where there was no one."

Helen shivered, she had never been fond of scary stories. "Walter, is it really necessary to discuss this now?   It seems silly to discuss ghosts in the dark sitting around a fire."

"Oh, buck up," Frederick spoke before Helen could say anything else. "Why do girls always have to be such fraidy-cats?"

Walter leaned down to whisper into his girlfriend's ear. "Don't worry, darling. I would never let a ghost near you. You are safe with me."

Twisting herself around, Helen let Walter kiss her softly. "I appreciate the sentiment."

"Look, I need to go make certain all is well up at the light. I'll be back in a jiff and then I have something very important to ask you." After another kiss, Walter headed for the lighthouse.

Helen's heart raced as she thought about what his statement could mean. She had waited a long time for these words and after the way they had left the last time, Helen finally felt like things were working out. Standing, she hurried over to the other couple, who were in the throes of a very intimate kiss, and grabbed her friend's hand interrupting them.   Clara grumbled while Helen dragged her friend away from a frustrated Frederick.

"Honestly Helen, what is this about?" Clara asked when they stopped near the edge of the woods that lined the west side of the lighthouse.

"I think Walter's going to propose tonight," Helen burst out.

"What?   How do you know?"

"He said he had something important to ask me when he comes back from checking on the light.   What else could it be?"

The girls squealed in unison, hugging each other.   In a flash, Helen could picture life here at Big Bay Point Light.   Winters curled up with Walter as her husband, knitting him warm sweaters to wear while fending off the harsh cold.   Children scurrying around the grass in the wind coming off of Lake Superior during the summer.

"I'm so happy for you!" Clara said once the two calmed down.   Something caught Clara's eye over Helen's shoulder.   "Speaking of which, it looks like the man of the hour is waiting for you."   She nodded and Helen turned around.

Down toward the water, partially hidden by the trees, stood Walter.   He was too far away to be seen clearly and cast in darkness from the woods, but his red hair danced wildly around his head, catching the bright flash of the lighthouse.

Excitement coursed through Helen's veins.

"Congratulations," Clara said, hugging her friend once more.

Helen started off toward her boyfriend, possibly soon to be fiancée. He turned into the woods before she reached him, and she slipped in between the trees to follow. Anywhere Walter went, she would surely go. No matter how fast she hurried, it seemed impossible to catch up with him. He wasn't running, he didn't even seem to be walking that quickly but she could never get near. At steady intervals, light shone through the trees lighting the way.

"Walter, wait for me."

The wind rushed through the trees and his answer danced around Helen. "Come."

Helen burst through the trees where Walter had gone. Her momentum threw her forward and she stumbled, coming to a halt at the edge of a cliff. Swinging her arms for balance, she took a step back to stop herself from plummeting over the rock and into the deadly water below. Heart thundering in her chest, Helen clutched her stomach as she stared down into the black lake. She took another few steps back. The excitement she had felt earlier vanished, leaving behind an upset stomach.

"I have missed you." The words were whispered from behind her. She turned around. Standing there was a man with bright red hair, who was not her Walter. His face was expressionless but she couldn't focus on his features, his entirely white eyes took her attention. She took a step back to get away from the man but stopped when she remembered the cliff edge was already precariously close to where she stood.

"Who are you?   What do you want?" Her voice was barely above a whisper, her throat felt restricted. She could barely breathe.

The man's hair continued to blow around his face though there was no wind. "My own wife does not recognize me?" His voice was soft but sincere, deeper than Walter's, and seemed to carry the wind with it.

Helen's heart froze before beating faster. He was blocking her from leaving, and she wanted nothing more than to be back at the fire. "I am certainly not your wife, I can help you find her if you back away. Please, you're scaring me."

"Why didn't you wait for me, Mrs. Prior? We can be together again."

The recognition set in and froze her blood. "William Prior?"

His white eyes blinked. "I have missed you."

He was dead. He died almost ten years ago. How was he standing in front of her?

Someone called her name in the distance. "Helen, Helen where are you?"

She opened her mouth to yell back, to call for help. But no sound came.

William Prior stepped closer to Helen, pulling her attention from her friends' call. "Why didn't you wait for me?"

His face was only inches from her, white eyes glowing, reflecting everything and nothing. The wind that stirred around him played with her hair. He smelled like crisp autumn leaves and the cold lake. There was nothing but silence about him, as she stared into his blank eyes all sound disappeared but the crashing waves below.

"I am not your wife," Helen whispered, it was a challenge to speak even quietly. "Please, let me go back to my friends."

The ghost flickered, momentarily turning iridescent. "We can be together again."

The wind picked up into a fierce gale that swept Helen off her feet and over the edge of the bluff toward the dark water's waiting embrace.

As she fell to her death, Helen thought, *I wonder how long Walter will wait for me?*

Snowballs

By Evelyn M. Zimmer

Snow. Gazing out the window, deep in thought Alaxia watched the first flakes of snow for the season as they gently blanketed the landscape. A steaming cup of hot apple cider with fresh cinnamon scented the air as it sat next to her untouched on the table, her attention on the gentleman that was just leaving through the gate. He paused outside the gate, looking back over his shoulder he thought he caught a glimpse of her in the window, but then the light changed and he continued on his way.

Alaxia continued to gaze out the window as a memory assaulted her causing her to nearly giggle out loud. It was years ago, as she was approaching adulthood, her parents were still alive, it was before the world changed, before she changed. Picking up a Christmas cookie she dipped it in the cider and nibbled delicately as she let her memories return.

It was during a family holiday vacation in Frankenmuth. The snow was enchanting and everyone was filled with a free and cheerful spirit. The town always looked like a little Bavaria, but in the winter, it was transported to another time. The local children were trying to make a buck by selling premade snowballs for those to slow or lazy to create their own cashes as well as refreshment stands for those that wished to observe instead of participate. In the air hung the ever present scent of chicken cooking, especially in the park so close to both Zehnder's and the Bavarian Inn. It was time for the battle of battles...the adults against the children. The annual snowball fight was a tradition that all held dear.

Alaxia was still a year away from finally joining the enemy...the adults! She and her sisters as well as many of the other 'children' had been making snowballs for days and hiding them in strategic spots all around the perimeter of the town. Makeshift barricades where erected as well as snowman sentinels...it was truly a magical time. The Mayor and both his sons, Richard and Quinn were on the side of the adults with her parents.

Her little sister Dianna was readying her trusty slingshot and aiming squarely for their father when Eva placed a hand on her arm to stay the shot, "Not papa" she giggled, "Alaxia wants us to take out Quinn first...she owes him for the dunk in the lake!"

"Really? Is she still holding that grudge? But he asked for it!" Exasperated Dianna changed her target, she herself wanted to pelt papa for grounding her just because she snuck out of the house to trap that rabbit...how was she supposed to now it was gonna be a gift?

Alaxia had a stash of snowballs ready and at her feet, she was warming up her pitching arm when all of a sudden she let it fly, pummeling him in the chest, followed quickly by Dianna's shot from her sling and Eva missed, but it still exploded on the tree trunk near his head. Dropping his snowball Quinn charged the girls-arms flailing in a silly imitation of a demon and as the two younger girls scattered behind the barricades, Alaxia's backside came up against the short snowy wall, she was trapped and braced herself for the inevitable.

Quinn came crashing down upon her, tackling her backwards over the barrier and landing down on top of her as her hands came up smashing snow into his face and giggling like a child caught in the cookie jar. Quinn braced himself above her on his hands, his knee between her legs trapping her and he shook his head roughly sending snow and slush all over her. His laugh was pure magic for her, time stood still for a half second as their eyes met...merriment on their faces, pink cheeked from the cold and exertion, and in his eyes...something more...a promise of a future.

Her smile froze as his head bent low, coming closer to hers, she was sure this was it, this was going to be her first kiss...but nothing happened. Her father cleared his throat from a distance and the Mayor slapped papa on the back and they both chuckled and began to pelt us both with snowballs. Quinn growled low in his throat and sprang to his feet, helping her up with a courtly gesture, he then picked her up over his shoulder and tossed her into the barricade bring it down upon her sisters...The battle of the children against the adults was still raging strong...Alaxia couldn't help but keep him within targets range, yet she never pelted him again...

"Want a warm up Alaxia?" Eva asked as she brought in a fresh pot of cider and several more cups. Noticing the additional cups, Alaxia tore her gaze away from the window and smiling happily she spoke nearly to herself. "It's nice that some of the families are still here..."

About the Authors

Caitlin Siem

Caitlin Siem is a writer of all things fiction. She has won multiple flash fiction competitions, been invited to read her poetry at local readings, and writes young adult novels. While living in Indianapolis, Indiana for a short time she co-founded a women's writing group. From Big Rapids, Michigan, Caitlin spends her time writing and enjoying everything Pure Michigan has to offer.

Edward Ahern

Ed Ahern resumed writing after forty odd years in foreign intelligence and international sales. He has his original wife, but advises that after forty five years they are both out of warranty. Ed has had forty seven stories published thus far. He dissipates his free time in German, French and Japanese language groups, fly fishing and shooting.

Edited by Evelyn M. Zimmer

James Vescovi

James Vescovi's writing has appeared in The New York Times, Creative Nonfiction, Newsday, Gazetta Italiana, Midwestern Gothic, the Georgetown Review and other places. *Eat Now; Talk Later (2014)* is the name of his memoir containing 52 stories about his nutty grandparents.

John Vicary

John Vicary began publishing poetry in the fifth grade and has been writing ever since. A contributor to many compendiums, his most recent credentials include short fiction in the collections "Midnight Circus", "We Were Heroes" and "Temporary Skeletons". John is the Submissions Editor at Bedlam Publishing. He enjoys playing piano and lives in rural Michigan with his family.

Evelyn M. Zimmer

Evelyn Zimmer began her writing career in the second half of her life. While she has always had a love affair with the written word, it wasn't until now that she has had the time to dedicate herself to her passion. In her spare time she enjoys various activities with her friends and visiting her family across the States. She lives in her family home in Michigan with her husband Paul and the newest addition to their family, a Shih-Tzu named Leo.

www.ingramcontent.com/pod-product-compliance
Lightning Source LLC
Chambersburg PA
CBHW070636130626
46555CB00006B/2564